THE FESTIVITIES OF MORKWOOD

E.J. BABB

Also by E.J. Babb:

These Unnatural Men

FOREGROUND

ABOUT THE AUTHOR

E.J. Babb lives in Southend-on-Sea with her partner, Carl Babb-Doherty, a couple of rescue dogs and a mischief of rescue rats. By day she is a copywriter, and by night, lunch break, weekend and bank holiday she is a blogger and author.

In 2012, E.J. Babb created her website, Dystopic (www.dystopic.co.uk), to openly revel in the devastatingly savage yet perpetually hopeful world of dystopian fiction.

Her debut novel, *These Unnatural Men*, was released in 2018. Her collection of five short stories, *FOREGROUND*, was released in 2020.

For Rachael, who loves the spooks just as much as I do.

1st DECEMBER

I hate Christmas.

The tacky decorations. The irritating, repetitive songs. The forced cheeriness. The bland food that swells in your stomach.

The build-up throughout December is nothing but an empty promise culminating in bitter disappointment. And it's worse in Morkwood, the village I live in. You've probably never heard of us – only neighbouring villages tend to recognise the name. And no one ever visits or travels through, because Morkwood is a dead end in the corner of nowhere.

Christmas is a real community event in Morkwood. It has to be – it's against local law for villagers to refuse to take part. It's one of those old, very English bylaws that no one has thought to get rid of. A few remain in London – pregnant women are allowed to urinate in police helmets, for example, and you're not allowed to flag down a taxi if you have the plague.

In Morkwood, all villagers must participate in opening the doors of the Advent House.

The tradition began one hundred and fifty years ago with Lord Bartholomew Greville, the son of a penniless gambling addict. Greville somehow managed to marry rich, and with his newfound money bought all the land in Morkwood and built an enormous manor house on the outskirts of the village.

One summer, Greville hired some local carpenters to build a wooden advent calendar. He intended it to be the size of a dollhouse and filled with twenty-four gifts for his two young daughters in the lead-up to Christmas.

The lord was adamant about designing the thing himself – local records detail several occasions of where he referred to the villagers as 'halfwits' – yet in his plans, the measurements were written down incorrectly. Perhaps he wrote metres instead of centimetres, or there was some form of sabotage, I don't know, there are a lot of conflicting accounts as to what happened. Either way, the carpenters he hired didn't doublecheck the plans with the lord and spent months making a huge advent calendar the same height as the manor house. The structure completely covered the side of the it, like a huge wooden extension.

Lord Greville was travelling around Europe with his family while the carpenters worked. When he returned and the Advent House was revealed to him, it's said he pretended it was exactly what he had wanted. Rather than a gift for his daughters, he proclaimed it was a gift for the whole village. A way to bring everyone together at a special time of year.

Many of the villagers believed him. Most worked in farms owned by the lord, so rumours began to circulate of pay rises and cooked hams waiting behind the doors. When Lord Greville announced the Advent House was to be an annual obligation for anyone with a Morkwood address, the villagers assumed it was because of contractual or tax reasons.

Lady Greville was an amateur artist, and her husband commissioned her to paint twenty-four backgrounds to go behind each of the doors. The paintings slid out at the back, so the order could be changed each year. However, much to the disappointment of the villagers, it was the paintings themselves that were the gifts – each one an activity or challenge for the village to do together. There were no hams, and certainly no pay rises. According to local documents, this led to a small-scale riot that cost three people their lives. Unsurprisingly, this part isn't mentioned when the villagers retell the story to their children.

So that's what we do each year in Morkwood. We get together every single day for twenty-four days and perform the same activities and challenges, all because a rich man wanted to save face over a century ago.

Today is the first of December. When the clock struck midnight, I poured myself two fingers of whisky and downed it in a single gulp. That is my own private tradition.

At half past twelve I pulled jeans over the top of my long johns, slipped my boots on and went out into the cold and dark and wet and miserable to traipse through the village to the manor house. The day of the month corresponds with the time each door is opened, so for the first of December it's opened at one in the morning, for the second it's two o'clock, and so on. It's another exhausting element to the whole thing.

Most of the villagers were standing in a semi-circle around the Advent House by the time I arrived, shrouded in a hum of excited chatter. A few like to dress up in old fashioned clothes and carry flaming torches on the first day, but most, like me, just wore whatever was warm and used the light on their phones to guide the way.

I waved to a couple of people but made sure to stand near the back. I generally like to keep out of the way of village activities.

"Good morning, Margaret."

I turned to see my Aunt Iris, dressed in a waterproof jacket and muddy jodhpurs, standing beside me. She had a battery-powered torch in her hand and a scowl on her face.

"It begins again," I said.

"It does indeed. The year gets shorter every year."

I nodded, too cold to laugh politely at her favourite saying. "What do you think it'll be today?"

"Who knows. I just hope it isn't the lake."

William Greville, a descendant of Lord Greville, made his way to the front of the crowd, clapping his gloved hands to quieten everyone down. As a Greville, he's exempt from proceedings and only has to open the doors, a technicality he pretends to be disappointed about.

"Welcome, everyone. It's always lovely to see you dressed in your fineries and excited for Christmas. Before I start, is anyone missing?"

People glanced over their shoulders. A few pointed fingers attempted to count the crowd.

"We're all here!" someone called out.

"Good," William said, "that's what I like to hear. We don't want to force everyone to sign a register like we did in '93 – that took bloody forever. And let's keep things nice and calm as well, shall we? Let's not push and pull, we don't want another broken arm, do we Arthur?"

There were woops and giggles as Arthur, a forty-something man with slicked-back hair and a paunch, gave a dramatic bow. Arthur is a fairly ruthless person, but he's even more so in December. He works in a small insurance firm outside of Morkwood and thinks of himself as some sort of high-flying investment banker rather than the small-fly car insurance salesman he actually is.

Thankfully, William doesn't enjoy giving long speeches like his father used to. He wasted no time in walking straight over to the first door of the Advent House, which was on the bottom right-hand side. A large '1' was carved into the wood. He took off one of his gloves and put his bare hand on the door handle, unable to suppress the grin on his face as he watched the crowd go completely still. Even the Harris' new-born baby was uncharacteristically silent.

William twisted the door handle and slowly pulled the door towards him.

"Merry Christmas!" he shouted into the thick silence.

As William stepped back, I stood on my tiptoes to see over the heads of the people in front of me. I could just about see the painting inside, which was of six or seven prepubescent boys, all pink-faced with dark blond hair, holding red prayerbooks in front of them and wearing stark white albs. Their small mouths were open in an 'o' shape, and their large blue eyes were wide and worried-looking.

I let out the breath I had been holding.

"Wonderful!" William said in mock surprise, even though we all knew he had chosen the order of the advent paintings. "So today we will sing. Mrs Lassiter, would you be so kind as to conduct?"

Mrs Lassiter, a tiny, frail old lady who was once in charge of the church choir, shuffled to the front. She was wearing a brown Victorian dress that was far too big for her and looked as though it was in the process of swallowing her whole. She pulled her bonnet back a little so she could wince at the sea of faces in front of her, and then held up a withered, veiny hand.

"One, two, three…"

Come on, haste, let us open,
The Advent House doors await.
Wake up the children, wrap up warm,
Quick, best not be late.

For if we delay, no matter why,
The woods will know it first.
The trees will find and claim us,
And our Yule-tide will be curs'd.

And if we refuse the games and folly,
Thoust surely misunderstood.

There is fear in the night for those who scorn
The festivities of Morkwood.

There was applause. William and Mrs Lassiter merged back into the crowd as it descended upon tables of mulled wine and mince pies like a swarm of ants. I stayed where I was. All I wanted to do was go home and down another two fingers of whisky.

I looked at Aunt Iris, who wasn't making any moves towards the tables either.

"While I do hate singing," she said, "I'm glad it wasn't the lake."

I sighed, because the lake is still to come. It's sitting behind one of those doors.

I looked back over to the happy crowd. Each year it surprises me how quickly they forget. It always starts off easy like this, but there's still twenty-three doors left to open.

2nd DECEMBER

It felt as though only a few hours had passed before I was looking up at the Advent House again, the taste of whisky in my mouth.

The atmosphere felt different this morning. More subdued. As if it had suddenly dawned on the rest of Morkwood that there were twenty-three days left of this. We all knew what was coming, it was just a matter of when.

William was no less jovial than he was yesterday. His white teeth were positively shining against his flushed complexion as he rocked back and forth on his heels, checking his watch intermittently. The door would be opened not a minute later – and certainly not a minute sooner – than two o'clock.

At around ten minutes to two, William spotted Mrs Lassiter in the crowd. He beckoned her over and stooped to whisper something in her ear.

The entire village quietly watched this exchange. After he had finished speaking, Mrs Lassiter nodded, briefly touched William's elbow, and retreated around the side of the crowd. She stopped a few feet from where I was standing, right at the very back. It was clear to all what had just happened.

William had told Mrs Lassiter what was behind the door.

There was a ripple of movement as people began to shift their weight from foot to foot, stretch their legs and generally warm their freezing bodies. As Mrs Lassiter had been advised to steer clear of the rest of the villagers, it could mean only one thing: we were going to have to run.

"Good morning, everyone," William said.

He knew exactly what he had done by speaking to Mrs Lassiter so brazenly. He surveyed the villagers with his hands on his hips, revelling in the commotion he had caused.

"We're all here, aren't we? Good, that's what I like to see. Don't forget, I'm good friends with the Christmas elves – I have eyes and ears everywhere."

William had to use the cherrypicker to reach this morning's door. He put on a hard hat and slowly ascended to the centre of the top row. Once he was close enough, he reached forward and took hold of the door handle.

"Merry Christmas!" he yelled, and flung the door open.

A few villagers raised binoculars, but from the pattern of blurred shapes I knew immediately which painting it was.

It was of a family of four, a mother, father, son and daughter. They were all sprinting towards a wooden bench on the left-hand side of the painting. The mother had bunched her dress up above her knees. The daughter was right behind her, flinging her boots into the air so she could run in bare feet. The father was in the process of pushing the son to the ground with an outstretched arm. Each of the painted faces were frozen in panic.

It took mere seconds for the chaos to begin.

Small children were thrown over shoulders. Men and women began to tackle one another to the ground and elbow each other out the way. Older members of the community tried to avoid the scuffle, but few succeeded. There were screams and cries as the whole crowd pushed and jostled and heaved.

And then, as if they had suddenly amalgamated into one giant being, the crowd began sprinting as one towards the centre of the village.

Today's game was the church dash. The aim is to get to a pew at the village church before every space is taken. It can only seat around three-quarters of the population of Morkwood, if that, and anyone who doesn't get a seat has to run a lap of the village.

I took a few steps back to avoid the stampede. In its wake were a trail of dishevelled bodies lying in the mud, some already scrambling to get back up. Others had decided to stay still until it was safe.

I waited until most of the villagers had gone before picking up the fallen. There were a few other villagers who had also chosen to stay behind to give the elderly and lesser abled a fighting chance. There was the young doctor, the postman and a few of the farmers, but the majority of those under the age of sixty had gone.

And for what? What was so terrible about taking a lap of the village if you were able to? My mother once told me it was the thought of losing that made them run so frantically, but it's not that. I know it's not that.

They're animals. All of them. Dumb, mindless, heartless animals.

As I turned to usher the stragglers towards the church, I bumped into William. He had an arm around Mrs Lassiter, and she was looking up at him like a dumb, obedient dog.

"I suppose you better get ready to run that lap," he said.

At that moment I wanted nothing more than to pick up a rock and plunge it into the softest part of his face.

3rd DECEMBER

"The doctor said he was surprised I didn't break it."

Dan Hewett, Joan and Harold's eldest, held his swollen wrist aloft for all to see.

"It's only sprained," Harold said matter-of-factly.

"A *bad* sprain, the doctor said."

"Still only a sprain."

Dan shrugged and stared, mesmerised by his wrist. It was the first year his parents had permitted him to run the church dash by himself, and he seemed to view his subsequent injury as a badge of honour.

Dan's best friend, Jack, tried to poke the spongey flesh with his forefinger. Dan laughed and slapped him away with his good hand.

We were all trudging slowly through the thick, wet mud at half past three this morning. Today's door had been the painting of a Christmas tree, so we immediately followed William into the woods to find a tree to cut down and decorate. There were no real rules with this activity, only that William had to pick the tree and it had to be cut using the traditional method of a two-man crosscut saw. William would also decide which two men (and it was always men) would do it.

I was aching from yesterday's run and not in the best of moods. My exercise usually consists of walking to and from the library for work, or the occasional stroll to the pub or greengrocers. God knows how Mrs Lassiter and my aunt feel – I imagine they must have walked for the majority of their laps, but I had seen both attempt to jog at the very beginning. Mrs Lassiter is at least ninety, so it's a miracle she's still alive.

"Did you get a seat yesterday, Margaret? I didn't see you there."

Lucy, the owner of the Purple Petal café, had somehow materialised by my side. She was the year above me in school and has always tortured me in the most mundane, senseless of ways. Her smile makes my teeth clamp together.

"No, Lucy, you know I didn't."

"Don't tell me, you didn't bother trying again."

"No, I did not."

"Was it because you knew you wouldn't get a seat, even if you did try?"

"Yes, that's exactly it. You are revoltingly intelligent, as always."

As Lucy opened her mouth to retort, the people in front of us came to a sudden halt.

William had chosen a tree.

I can't have been the only one to feel confused. The tree in front of us was thick, but not very tall – not much more than six feet. And yet William patted the trunk as though it were the neck of a handsome horse.

"Ladies and gentlemen, say hello to this year's Morkwood Christmas tree, isn't she a beauty?"

That inspired the villagers to clap, as if William's choice suddenly made sense. I only joined in to not call attention to myself.

"And now it's time to pick our cutters. Mr Terrence Jordan, will you be the first to step up, please?"

There was more polite applause as Terry, a skinny, balding man who works in the hardware shop, came forward to pick up one end of the saw. I could tell he was beside himself with joy. He was a quiet, proud man and not often picked for community events – except for the cricket match every summer, for which he was always umpire.

"And now for our second cutter. Mr Daniel Hewett, could you please step forward?"

Of course he picked Dan. I don't know how I hadn't seen it coming.

There were mutterings as Dan stumbled to the front, holding his arm close to his chest, clearly bewildered to hear his name called. Joan pushed her way through the crowd after him.

"William, I'm so sorry, would you be able to pick someone else?" She stepped in front of her son. "As you can see, Dan has injured himself quite badly and I don't think he's be up to the job."

William snorted. "Well, well, well, Daniel. Your mother says you're not up to the job. I haven't done this in twenty-three years, but if you have to do what mummy says, I could always pick someone else…"

Dan looked disdainfully at his mother. "I'm fine, it's not even broken."

"But, Dan…"

"I said I'm *fine*."

Joan looked to Harold for support, but received nothing in return.

"That's settled then," William said. "Men, if you could grab the saw at each end, we'll get cutting."

Dan bent over to pick it up with his good hand.

"You'll need both hands for this, Daniel," William said.

Dan nodded. He picked it up with his good hand first, but as soon as the fingers on his injured hand wrapped around the saw handle, he immediately dropped it. He tried again and the same thing happened, only this time a pained grunt escaped his lips.

"How about Stanley," Terry offered. "Or Milo, or Niles, or…"

"I chose Daniel," William said.

Dan dropped the saw only one more time. Then he jutted out his chin and, with a strangled yell, forced himself to grip tightly onto the handle with both hands. He moved quickly towards the tree, his face reddening with the effort.

Terry looked like he was about to weep. "Dan, mate, maybe we should…"

"No," Dan said. Tears were falling down his cheeks as his whole body began to tremble.

Two hours. We all stood still and silent like the trees around us for two hours, listening to that boy sob as he slowly sawed through the bark, millimetre by millimetre. With each push and pull he winced and cried out, incapable of hiding his agony.

I closed my eyes, willing the tree to crash to the ground.

Just when I thought I couldn't take any more, I heard a snap and a low creak. As the sun began to rise, the tree finally made its descent.

4th DECEMBER

I don't know why I'm writing this diary, or if I'm expecting it to ever be read – I just feel a record has to be made. Each December the darkness seeps further into Morkwood, leaving a stain that is becoming increasingly difficult to conceal.

I don't ever want to get used to it the way the others have. The callous manner in which they stepped over Dan to get to the tree, Their singing, their *laughter*.

As we watched the children decorate the tree, Dan looked pale and exhausted. His father had to hold him up, he was so weak. By midday the swelling had spread and he was unable to bend his elbow.

When I saw Dan again this morning as the fourth door was opened, his arm was supported by a sling and he was still horrendously ashen-faced. But he smiled with relief when he saw the advent painting – a group of men toasting over a fireplace.

This activity would be enjoyable for him, at least.

Kenneth Rowley hobbled towards the pub to open the doors. We gave him ten minutes before following suit and queuing for our shots of schnapps.

With the comforting glow of the pub up ahead, it was almost possible to forget we were taking part in the Morkwood Advent House – that was, until the Harris' new-born baby began screaming.

"It's a lot though, isn't it? Can't we give him the other half later?"

I don't know what Carla Harris expected Kenneth to say.

After gurgling and more screaming, Carla scurried back towards the direction of her cottage, a little bundle of blankets thrashing and wailing in her arms. The queue moved forward.

This has to stop.

5th DECEMBER

The rumours began yesterday. The villagers always think they can predict which door William will choose next.

"He picks the fire around this time."

"No, it'll be the lake."

"Are you kidding? It's far too early. It's going to be the bedtime one."

"He does that nearer to Christmas Day."

"Not true. Five years ago he did it on the ninth."

"Oh, yeah, I forgot about that."

On and on and on it went. The library is a hub for idle gossip in Morkwood, particularly with the older members of the community. They can often be found milling around the romance or history sections, speaking far too loudly about things I don't want to hear.

Mabel Lundt, a despicable blabbermouth, even tried to get me to join in.

"I reckon Margaret knows," Mabel said, nudging her friend Junie in the ribs.

I held my hand out so I could stamp her copy of *Lord of Scoundrels*, but she held it close to her chest, goading me to speak.

I relented. "Why would I know which door is next?"

"You're quiet."

"So?"

"The quiet ones always know more than they let on," Junie butted in excitedly, no doubt parroting words she had heard coming out of Mabel's mouth.

I sighed. "I don't know anything. Now, are you going to let me stamp your book, or are you going to stand here all day wasting my time?"

The truth is, there is a discernible pattern to the paintings William chooses, insofar as he does everything possible to subvert expectations. Sometimes the activity will be the opposite of what the villagers expect to see, and other times he does exactly what was predicted, because no one will be expecting that. It's an endless mind game.

I try not to drive myself to distraction thinking about the Advent House all day, but it's difficult not to. And that's exactly what William wants.

As the door was being opened at five o'clock this morning, I decided to go to bed early last night to wake up at four, but it was hard to fall asleep. I had to keep reminding myself to relax my jaw, unfurl my balled fists and stop taking note of every little noise in the house. The Advent House makes me paranoid. I feel as though William is lurking somewhere in the darkness, waiting to catch me out with an unscheduled activity just as I let my guard down.

When I finally fell asleep, I was woken less than an hour later by the shrill beeping of my alarm clock. I arrived at the Advent House with barely seconds to spare, completely disoriented.

"You're pushing it," Aunt Iris said as I stumbled up beside her. "You know what happens when people turn up late. And what if you'd missed it entirely? Jesus, I daren't even think about that..."

"But I didn't miss it, did I?" I said, trying to catch my breath. "I'm here."

"Only just. It's not worth the risk, is all I'm saying."

But as it turned out, I didn't even need to be there. Today's painting was of a small, half-built wooden structure with men dotted around the outside carrying axes, hammers and small planks of wood.

"Women and children, go home immediately," William ordered, sticking his chest out as if becoming engorged with his own self-importance. "All the men need to make their way to the village hall."

During the first ever year of the Advent House, this painting instigated the creation of the Morkwood village hall. All the men built it together, and they worked around the clock to get it finished in time for Christmas. Every year since, whenever the painting has been revealed, the men of Morkwood spend time working on its repairs.

The village hall is where all major social gatherings happen, from christenings to wakes. It's also where everyone gathers after church on Christmas Day.

There was a sense of disappointment from the crowd, especially from the children, but I was more than happy to turn around and go straight back home.

Yet, for the entirety of the walk back, I couldn't stop thinking about that damned Advent House. Why did the repairs only never take a couple of hours every year? Why were all the men sullen and distracted beforehand, and even quieter when they emerged afterwards? Come to think of it, what repairs had they even needed to do?

Just two weeks ago, William hired workmen from outside of Morkwood to retile the toilet. He had asked everyone to donate money towards it.

In spring, outsiders had been hired to repaint the interior walls.

Why would William hire professionals to do the sort of jobs the Morkwood men could complete over Christmas?

When I reached my doorstep, I knew I had to go to the village hall and take a look. It would eat me up for the rest of the year if I didn't.

I watched the women and children return to their homes from my front window. I waited until the lights were turned off in their homes, switched off my own and then quietly crept out.

It was still quite dark, so I don't think anyone could have seen me as I made my way towards the village hall. I used memory and the faint early morning light to guide me.

I approached the hall from the back to keep myself hidden, but fortunately the men were already inside.

The village hall windows are quite high, but there was a mop and bucket propped against the back door. I upturned the bucket and placed it beneath one of the windows. I still had to stand on tiptoes to see inside, but I only wanted a brief look.

Clinging to the wall for support, I just about got my nose over the window ledge. In the hall, the men of the village were quietly chatting with one another, and as the windows were so old I could hear almost every word they were saying.

William was standing on the stage, of course, waiting for the perfect time to take control of proceedings. And it wasn't long before he opened his mouth to bellow out commands.

"All right, all right, gents. It's time. We don't have anyone new here, do we? No fresh-faced eighteen-year-olds? Okay then, you know what to do. Let's get this over with."

I don't know what I expected to happen, but I almost fell off the bucket when the men began unzipping their coats, pulling their jumpers over their heads and kicking off their shoes.

One by one they stripped down, completely naked, and piled their clothes near the entrance to the hall.

William remained clothed. He waited until every single man was undressed, and then grabbed a couple of large shopping bags.

"Pass these around, will you?" he said to Terry, who was standing at the foot of the stage.

I tried not to look at Terry's scrawny body as he reached up to take the bags from William and placed them on the floor. He then pulled out an armful of what looked like small planks of wood – some with twigs glued to the top of them, others without.

The men came forward and each took a piece of wood from Terry. It took a while for everyone to get one, but there was more than enough to go around.

"Are we all sorted?" William asked.

I noticed he hadn't taken one for himself.

"Okay, now put them on."

That's when I realised what they were. Small, wooden masks. Some of them had stag-like horns attached to the top. There seemed to be no logic behind why some men had masks with horns and others didn't.

My lack of sleep numbed me to the sheer ridiculousness of the sight before me. Here were all the men of Morkwood, standing naked in the village hall wearing masks. And then there was William at the front like an insane conductor.

"All right, gentlemen," he said. "Arms up."

They all raised their arms above their head, as if on a rollercoaster.

Suddenly one of my feet slipped off the bucket. I grabbed onto the window ledge to retain my balance.

And then I looked up.

William was staring straight at me.

I jumped off the bucket and crouched down low, breathing heavily, trying to work out where to run to. If William came out the back, I could go into the woods and hide. If he came out the front I could try and make it home, but the sun was coming up and he'd definitely see me.

Had he even recognised me? Why was I so frightened? What did I think he was going to do to me?

And what were *they* about to do?

I waited.

No one came out of the village hall.

Maybe he hadn't seen me. Maybe light was reflecting off the glass and it had obscured me from view.

But what if he had?

"Fuck it," I said under my breath.

I ran straight back to the house.

6th DECEMBER

I didn't sleep at all last night. I was going over and over what happened in my head, trying to figure out the likelihood of William having seen me. If he had, surely he would have left the village hall? Or spoken to me later in the day. He's not one to leave things unsaid.

He didn't speak to me, but that doesn't mean he doesn't know that I saw…whatever it was I saw.

The wooden masks looked like something a child would have made, simple and roughly cut. Why were all the men wearing them, and why were they naked with their arms above their heads? Was it a sexual thing? I can't imagine Terry or Lawrence or Victor – or even William come to think of it – allowing anything sordid to take place in Morkwood, even if it was in the name of tradition.

Still, tradition seems to nullify any act deemed obscene, pointless or cruel.

When I arrived at the Advent House this morning, I decided it would be easier not to look or speak to anyone. I'm not a very good liar, and the villagers of Morkwood seem to have a sixth sense when it comes to thinly veiled secrets. I wanted to talk to Aunt Iris first. I thought perhaps she might know what they'd been doing in the hall, or at least how I could find out.

I was so focused on not looking at anyone in the crowd that I didn't notice William open the door.

Everyone began to moan about whatever it was, but I couldn't see through the crowd. I searched for gaps in between heads, trying not to let my imagination get the better of me.

A couple of people stepped to the side, and then there it was. The painting of a dead, grey fish.

"Line up, ladies and gents!" William shouted.

There was confused toing and froing as everyone organised themselves shoulder to shoulder in a long line.

"You know the rules," William said as the commotion died down. "No moving. Not even a smile, including all you little ones. Are we ready? Three…two…one…freeze!"

I willed my body not to tremble in the cold, or react to the thoughts bombarding my mind. I regretted not putting my hands in my pockets during the countdown, or tucking my chin to my chest.

William walked slowly from one end of the line to the other, studying each of us from head to toe. I held my breath.

He was just a few feet away when Carla's baby kicked out, forcing her to tighten her grip on him.

My heart sank for her, but at the same time I was relieved it was over.

William marched straight up to me, grinning.

"Margaret Trellers!" he bellowed.

I don't remember exactly what I said, but I know it was cowardly. I think I started stuttering about Carla, trying to get William to believe that it was *her* who had moved first, not me. But he ignored my pleas.

"Wait here," he said, smirking. "I'll go get your prize."

William disappeared down the side of the Advent House. He came back with a cool box.

"It wasn't me," I said as he put it down in front of me. "It wasn't *me*. Why won't you listen?"

He put a hand up to shush me. "You know the rules. The first person to move has to eat it. All of it."

"But I didn't..."

"Quiet."

William lifted the lid off the cool box and pulled out a plastic bag from inside. He held it up for everyone to see.

Slumped at the bottom of the bag was a dead, uncooked fish coated in a thick layer of jelly.

"I didn't move first," I said. "You know I didn't."

I had intended my voice to sound accusatory, or even stern, but it came out as more of a whine. But the truth didn't matter anyway. He had chosen me. He had chosen me because of what I had seen.

William opened the bag and immediately turned his head to the side, grimacing at the smell. He thrust the thing into my chest.

The stench spread outwards like a cloud, getting stronger and stronger as I held the open bag. The people either side of me in the line took a few steps back, spluttering as the stench of rotten flesh filled the air.

The Advent Fish is left for a few weeks to ferment before being coated in a jelly made of animal fat and fish guts. Traditionally, the Advent Fish was a prize for whoever managed to stay still the longest, but the rules changed when modern tastes depicted the prize to be more of a punishment.

"I can't," I said, feeling the bile rise up in my throat.

I felt the eyes of Morkwood on me. I knew what they were all thinking. I would have thought the same thing too if it was someone else holding the bag: *just eat it*. Get it over with. It will be so much worse if you prolong the inevitable.

I swallowed the acidic taste in my mouth and put my hand in the bag, wrapping my fingers around the cold, slippery head of the fish. I felt my fingers sink deep into the jelly as I pulled it out.

Closing my eyes, I put the head in between my teeth and bit down.

The jelly exterior was fishy and salty, but it wasn't until my teeth touched the scales that I began to gag. I kept swallowing the jelly to try and calm the retching, but the cold blubber just kept coming back up into my mouth as my stomach lurched uncontrollably.

I swallowed hard, forcing it all back down.

Just a few minutes and it would all be over with. Just a few minutes.

I quickly realised the best tactic was to go as fast as possible. I started taking huge bites out of the fish, chewing as fast as I could, feeling the tiny bones splintering and crunching and imbedding into my teeth. The skin was chewy and hard to tear off, but it was the eyes that were by far the worst. Each one popped in my mouth, spilling thick, bitter liquid into my cheeks.

I tried to avoid identifying the specific parts I was eating – the fins, the lungs, the bowels – but my tongue inadvertently touched them all.

I made the mistake of opening my eyes as I neared the end, and I looked down at the gnawed mess in my hand. The thing that I was eating, mushed grey and red and purple, and the texture...the *smell*. I looked up at the sky, begging my body to hold it all in.

And then, finally, it was all over.

I didn't wipe my face on the sleeve of my coat, clean my hands on my trousers, or even think about how sick I felt. I just had to get away. I turned and started walking back to my house, one step at a time, one foot in front of the other.

I heard a few laughs and some cheers behind me, but I couldn't think about them. I couldn't imagine what they were about to say about me, or what they were going to say to me the next day. I just had to get home.

The second my front door was closed behind me, warmed, churned jelly spewed from my mouth and onto the floor, followed by whole chunks of flesh and shattered bone.

When the retching finally stopped, there was no question of what I had to do.

I had to ruin Christmas.

7th DECEMBER

Yesterday was my day off from the library. It took me a while to clean the vomit from my living room floor. The smell was almost unbearable, and it lingered. Afterwards I ran a bath and sat in it until it grew cold, then went to bed. By the time I woke up, it was dark outside.

I didn't leave the house. I didn't see anyone. I didn't speak to anyone. I didn't even want to risk hearing anyone, so I blocked out the world with earplugs and read until I was tired enough to go back to sleep.

I feel humiliated, not just because everyone saw me eat the fish, but because in the moment I felt I had no other choice but to do it. I can't recall ever seeing a villager refuse to take part in the Advent House, but what would have happened if I had said no? Nothing, most likely.

I'm also furious – at William for choosing me, and at myself for knowing full well that if Carla had been chosen, I would have simply watched her eat the fish. I wouldn't have tried to help her at all, like no one had tried to help me.

After witnessing that scene at the village hall, I'm now certain there's something hidden about this whole tradition. William chose me yesterday because he knew I had seen things I shouldn't have, but he also knows I haven't a clue what any of it means, and I'm not brave enough to speak out. The fish was a warning.

But William is just one man. At five o'clock this morning I realised that, if I was going to end the Advent House, I needed the villagers to be on my side. I quickly formed a plan. It wasn't a particularly well thought out one, but it was a plan nonetheless, so I got dressed and headed straight to the Advent House.

There was no one around at that time of the morning. I didn't expect there to be, but I stood right at the front anyway and I waited. I wanted them all to see me.

The villagers started to arrive at around half past six. I didn't say anything to them and stared straight ahead. No one said a word to me either. I think the mere sight of me at the Advent House so early and so close to the front was enough to make them wary of what I might do.

William arrived a little later than usual, just a few minutes before seven. I failed to catch his eye. I willed him to say something to me. A greeting. An offhand remark. Anything so I could bring up what I saw at the hall, but he avoided my gaze.

I had so much adrenaline pumping through my body I was quivering. I needed the painting behind the door to be something despised by everyone in Morkwood, like the lake or the elves, so I could turn to them all and ask if they thought it was normal to do this. If they thought this was *fun*. Did they think what I had to do yesterday, and what many people have had to do before me, was justifiable? Was it necessary?

But I didn't get my chance. William opened the door to reveal a painting of a grave covered in snow, and there was a collective dreamy sigh.

That's when he finally looked at me and smiled, as if he could see into my brain. As if he knew he had stopped something from happening.

By twenty past seven, we were all at the church. William told us to lie on the graves of the dead, look up at the grey-blue sky and think of the loved ones we weren't able to spend Christmas with.

I lay on the grave of my mother, Aislinn Trellers. But I didn't think of her. There is no longer any room in my head for sentimentalities. I need a better plan if I'm going to get the village on my side.

8th DECEMBER

The painting behind the door this morning was of a young girl. She's fair, perhaps aged ten or eleven, and has some sort of cream-coloured material covering her mouth that's tied at the back of her head. Her eyes are flat and dull. I've always thought she looks dead.

For twenty-four hours, everyone in Morkwood has to be silent. If anyone speaks, there will be an unpleasant forfeit.

Most years, the forfeits are bestowed on excitable children and vulnerable adults. No one is exempt from punishment.

Except for William, of course.

"Enjoy your day, everyone," William said as the villagers began to walk back to their homes.

Those who worked outside of Morkwood began emailing or texting their bosses, no doubt claiming a sudden bout of illness. Mothers put their fingers to their lips in an attempt to quieten their children – at least until they were out of earshot. And everyone else tread as carefully as possible, almost as if walking too fast might excite them into speaking.

But I didn't turn to leave with the rest of them. I remained in front of William and the Advent House, my hands in my pockets to hide the fact that they were shaking.

I filled my lungs with the painfully cold morning air.

"This is stupid," I said.

Perhaps the words I had chosen were not as profound as I'd have liked, but what can I say? I panicked.

I didn't need to look behind me to know that everyone had stopped in their tracks. For the first time that morning, William looked me in the eye, attempting to disguise his shock with a wry smile.

"Oh dear, Margaret," he said. "I'm sorry you feel that way. You better follow me. You too, Arthur, I'm going to need your help."

Arthur smoothed down his wet-looking hair and smirked as he pushed past me.

I followed William and Arthur into the woods. I had hoped some of the other villagers would come to watch, to keep me safe, but no one dared to. There was hot, sick feeling in the pit of my stomach, but I sunk my fingernails deep into my palms and willed myself to focus. I couldn't afford to be afraid. Not yet.

After what felt like a long time, William finally stopped in front of the stump where the Christmas tree had once stood.

"Take your shoes off," he ordered.

I took my boots and socks off, shuddering when the cold, wet mud slid between my toes.

"Now stand on the tree stump."

I stood on it.

"Stand on one foot."

"What?"

William huffed impatiently. "You heard me. I said stand on one foot."

I slowly lifted my left foot from the stump.

"Okay," William said. "I'll be back at noon. If you put that foot down, it's another four hours. Arthur will be here to keep an eye on you."

He started to walk back to the village, hesitated, then turned around again.

"Oh, and Arthur? Pick up that stick over there. No, not that one, the long one. Yes, that's it. Every time Ms Trellers speaks or puts her foot down, I want you to use that stick on the foot she's standing on."

William went to walk away again, but turned around one final time.

"By the way, Arthur, Ms Trellers has spoken twice so far."

William was barely a few metres away before Arthur lifted the stick high above his head. I felt his hot breath in my ear as he whispered, "You're the one who's stupid, Margaret."

9th DECEMBER

When I woke up this morning, I could feel that the wet, open wounds on the top of my right foot had fused with the bedsheet. I sat up and started to peel the fabric away as slowly and as gently as I could, but in the end I had no choice but to rip it off. It made my eyes water, and fresh blood dripped through to the mattress.

As I lowered my left foot to the ground, I yelped in pain – the aching muscles in that leg hurt just as much as the open wounds. I had held it aloft for a total of nine hours yesterday.

The image of Arthur's smug face materialised in my mind. To soothe myself, I imagined grabbing the stick out of his short, fat fingers and ramming it deep into the jelly of his eye.

Holding onto the walls for support, I limped to the kitchen to pour myself a glass of water. As I was wondering whether the pain of getting in the shower was worth it, I felt a jolt of panic – sunshine was streaming in through my kitchen window.

I looked to the clock on the wall.

Eight forty-five.

The ninth Advent House door was going to open in fifteen minutes. Even if I could somehow sprint the whole way, it would be impossible for me to get there in time.

But then a calmness washed over me.

"I'm not going," I said to myself, as if it were a vow I needed to say aloud in order to abide by it.

I picked up the telephone to tell Janice at the library that I wasn't going to work today, but then put it back on the cradle. No one would pick up. She was at the Advent House.

William won't let this go. And everyone will notice my absence. For a moment I considered barricading myself in by pushing the bookshelf in front of the door, but I quickly decided against that idea. Not only would it have been difficult with the pain I was in, but I never want William to think I'm frightened of him.

So I sat in my armchair, and I waited for him to come.

I've been waiting all day. I managed to eat a few bites of leftovers around lunchtime – it was all I could stomach – but aside from limping to the toilet a few times I've just been sitting, waiting.

It's dark outside now, and no one has come for me yet.

It's only a matter of time.

10th DECEMBER

No one took me in the night to punish me for going against the rules of the Advent House. No one even knocked.

Perhaps my absence had gone unnoticed. It was possible. I often stand at the back, and not all activities involve everyone in the village. Maybe I got away with it.

But that was unlikely. I began searching for clues in the house, anything broken or out of place, but I couldn't find anything. And since no one has visited me in almost five years now, I'm sure I would have noticed even the slightest of changes.

This morning I was supposed to be at the library by nine o'clock and then make my way to the Advent House for ten, but it seemed pointless working for less than an hour, so I went to work early. I also wanted to do a bit extra to apologise to my manager, Janice, for not working yesterday. Although I doubt she was rushed off her feet, she was probably a little annoyed that I wasn't there.

I put on my coat, boots and hat and limped to the front door. There was a light dusting of snow on the fields surrounding the house, and I felt a flutter of excitement. It would turn to slush by midday, but it lifted my spirits anyway. Snow always makes the world seem renewed.

I had been looking out at the frosty scene for quite a while before I noticed the footprints. They were slightly obscured by a thin layer of fresh snow, but I could just about see the edges of them. They started somewhere down the road, came in a straight line to my front gate, and then went down the garden path to my front doorstep. Finally, they veered off to the left and stopped by the fence.

I walked over to where the footprints ended. That's where, in amongst the long grass, I found a small, simple wreath made of twigs, ivy and twine. I picked it up but immediately dropped it again.

Woven into it were the severed body parts of a hare.

Its small, grey head and long, velvety ears were fastened at the top. The front legs stuck out at the sides and the back legs and tail were hanging off the bottom. What blood remained inside of the animal had frozen. The hare had been attached so that it looked as though the wreath had grown from within its stomach – twigs jutted out of its open mouth and eyes and ears and paws like a parasite overtaking its host.

I looked around but couldn't see the middle part of the hare, nor the person who had left it in my front garden.

"Hang the hang-ed hare on your door. Invite the curse inside. It'll eat you up, but you won't have to hide."

These are the words all Morkwood children are taught at Christmastime. It means the evil spirits will do terrible things, but they have a strict code to follow. If you abide by their rules, they'll do exactly what they say they'll do. If you don't, you're opening yourself up to endless, unknown fear.

Like Father Christmas, with his list of whose been naughty or nice, these threats are only real to children. I lifted the lid off my dustbin and dropped the wreath inside.

At the library, I worked quickly to stop myself from thinking about the fact that someone had been at my house, probably while I was asleep. Instead, I dusted shelves, swept the floors, put away returned books and organised displays. Finally, I tidied the kitchen and wrote a list of everything I had to do once I returned from the Advent House.

I left at the last possible moment, taking my time to lock up the library before hobbling to the Advent House. What if I was five, ten minutes late? What was the worst that could happen? Would I get another wreath? I don't want another poor creature to have to suffer, but I'd much rather go against the wishes of the village than allow this crazed tradition to continue.

Despite walking slowly, I arrived just in time for the opening of the door. William was in the cherrypicker, ascending to the second row from the top.

"Merry Christmas," he said, and pushed open the door.

I groaned.

The painting was of a grey lake. To the side of it was a wooden T-shaped structure, with one arm hanging over the water. At the end of the overhanging arm was a cage. Inside that cage was the grotesque figure of the shtriga, hunchbacked with teeth bared, excited to be drowned and reunited with the devil.

William looked down at us all, not even bothering to hide his excitement.

He took a deep breath and held up a crucifix. "If anyone here is shtriga, I command that you show yourself."

It is said that not even shtriga can lie to the lord, but Morkwood can't leave anything to chance. So as no one ever admits to being shtriga, every female over the age of thirteen has to follow William and Father Hundyke to the village hall. One by one our arms and legs are searched for the mark of the shtriga. Moles, warts, birthmarks, any sort of blemish could be a sign. If William decides he has found a mark, we go to the lake. If not, we go home.

At the lake, the woman accused of being shtriga is put in the wooden cage shown in the painting and is lowered into the water. If the woman floats, they are shtriga. If they sink, they're pulled out and everyone gets on with their day.

Everyone knows to hook their feet under the bottom of the cage when they're dunked, so no one is ever proven to be shtriga. There have been no deaths at the lake during my lifetime, but everyone always dreads it in case something goes wrong. The water must be *freezing*.

I decided I would volunteer to be checked first at the village hall, just to save time. I had a feeling William would find some sort of suspicious mark on my skin, so it was better not to delay the inevitable. At least I was dressed warmly.

"I am shtriga."

There were gasps as someone in the middle of the crowd raised their arm. In all my life, no one has ever called themselves shtriga. It's suicide.

"Come forward, shtriga," William said, seemingly unsurprised as he lowered the cherrypicker.

Everyone was pushing and shoving, both trying to let the shtriga through while at the same time grabbing her and pulling her around to show their disgust. I heard a few people shout 'traitor' and 'devil woman', and a few hacked up phlegm to spit at her.

By the time the shtriga had got to the front, she looked a bit dishevelled. Her coat was slipping off her shoulders and her white hair was falling out of its bun.

"Reveal yourself to the villagers you've deceived," William said, relishing every second.

The woman turned.

Aunt Iris.

The shtriga was Aunt Iris.

Without thinking I started to push my way through to the crowd, but unknown hands grabbed onto my shoulders and pulled me back.

"Aunt Iris!" I shouted, but she couldn't hear me above the yelling of the crowd.

The harder I pulled against the hands holding me, the firmer they held me in place. I could only watch as William led Aunt Iris around the side of the Advent House. They were going into the woods, with Father Hundyke not far behind.

"Stop!" I shouted.

"Thou shalt not suffer a witch to live," said one of the men holding me.

I managed to free an elbow. I rammed it hard into his face, but he retaliated with his fist. Everything went grey.

11th DECEMBER

I woke up yesterday evening in my bed, my face covered in dried blood.

They barricaded my bedroom door from the outside and nailed planks of wood across my window. There's no way I can get out.

I went to sleep again. I think I woke up in the early morning.

My diary was under my mattress, so I thought I might as well write.

I think I can hear them coming.

12th DECEMBER

It's still dark out. It'll be hours before the next door is opened, but I want to give myself enough time to write everything down.

They took me yesterday morning. William sent Arthur and Henry to fetch me. I begged them to tell me what was going on, but they wouldn't say a word. Henry's brow was furrowed the entire time, so I don't think he particularly wanted to be involved, but Arthur – he was holding himself back from doing something worse, I could tell.

I kept asking them about Aunt Iris. What had they done with her? Would they trial her at the lake to make sure she really was shtriga, or would they punish her straight away? Was she even alive? Why were they doing this?

But the two men said nothing as they tied my hands in front of me and pulled me down the stairs to the front door.

Outside, dozens and dozens of wreaths littered my front garden. Most of them had hares attached to them, but a few had crows or blackbirds. One had the head, legs and tail of a small brown cat.

The villagers had made them. It was their way of telling the evil spirits to come to my house, not theirs. It's beyond insane. They know the story, they *know* why the Advent House was created. An aristocrat used it to punish the poor villagers he despised so much, and had entwined old stories of spirits, demons and shtriga to add familiarity to the torture, but it was only ever a ruse to make one man feel powerful. And now it is William who feels that power.

How many Christmases will there need to be before they all realise it's the things they do that cause the pain, not the things they don't do?

Logic is not a currency I can barter with in Morkwood, so I allowed Arthur and Henry to march me through the empty village. I didn't put up a fight. I told myself I would know when it was time for that, but I had to conserve my energy.

At the Advent House, it felt like everyone in Morkwood turned at the same time to stare at me. And I stared right back. I wanted them to see me covered in my own blood, tired and hungry and exhausted. I wanted them to see what they were doing in the name of tradition.

I searched the crowd for Aunt Iris but I couldn't see her, only unsympathetic, vaguely familiar eyes. These were people I talked to at the library. People I had bought groceries from. People I had waved hello to on the street. Now they wanted hell to rain down on me because that meant nothing bad could happen to them.

"Idiots," I spat. Their expressions didn't change.

They're cattle, I thought. *Dumb, penned-in cattle.*

As William held up his hand to open the eleventh door, the cattle turned back to face their shepherd.

"I know it's almost lunchtime, so let's make this quick," William said, chuckling.

The painting behind the door was of men in dented top hats and women in shabby dresses, all holding hands in a circle, grinning inanely with one leg raised. A man in a fine morning suit played a fiddle around the outskirts of the circle.

"You know what that means!" William said, running to the side to grab his fiddle.

The eleventh day. That meant eleven minutes of dancing.

The villagers quickly sprang together to hold hands. Arthur and Henry tightened their grip on my elbows and pulled me in with them.

As William began to play a terrible rendition of My Wild Irish Rose, the villagers began to kick out their legs like marionette puppets. No one was really in time with the music, but that didn't matter – they just needed to move. Quickly.

William walked around the outside of the circle as he played, kicking the back legs of anyone who wasn't moving fast enough. When he got behind me, he booted my ankle so hard I toppled sideways into Henry.

"Dance the devil out, Margaret," he said. "You've already done Morkwood enough harm this year."

So I danced for him – well, if you could call what I was doing dancing. It felt like every movement scraped more and more layers of skin from the top of my injured foot, but I kept going. Every ounce of pain was directed straight at him

Once the eleven minutes were up, and another Advent House activity had ended, the villagers headed back to their jobs and their homes, flushed and breathless.

But Henry and Arthur held onto me, making it abundantly clear that I wasn't allowed to leave.

Once William had put his fiddle away, he said the five words I knew were coming.

"Take Margaret to the lake."

That's when I fought back. I threw my body from left to right and yanked my arms down as hard as I could to free myself. I kicked out at William and screamed and yelled, but I was too weak. I was no match for them. They pinned me to the ground and bound my feet with rope.

I continued to thrash about, and it took all three of them to carry me to the lake. Then Henry sat on me as the other two wheeled the wooden contraption out from behind the trees. I heard the metallic squeak as they opened the cage door, and then they pushed me inside.

Henry cranked a wheel and I was raised high into the air, dangling over the edge of the water.

Before I could even form the words to protest, I was plunged straight down into the grey depths of the lake.

The shock of the icy cold water forced a gasp out of me, but I managed to close my mouth before I swallowed too much water. I hooked my feet under the bars of the cage, just as my mother had taught me to do. I closed my eyes and held my breath.

Because I didn't float, the men were forced to pull me out again. I was not shtriga.

I coughed as soon as the air hit my face, bringing up the small amount of water I'd taken in. The men took their time pulling the contraption away from the water and getting me out of the cage. I shivered so violently from the cold my tongue was bitten and bleeding.

As I wrapped my arms closer around myself, my wet hair clinging to my face like seaweed, I wondered if Aunt Iris had also been inside that cage. I wondered if she had stepped out of it like I had, or whether they had dragged her lifeless body out.

Henry and Arthur took me straight back to my house, untied me and barricaded me in my bedroom. There were no thoughts in my head as I changed out of my wet clothes and wrapped myself up in my duvet.

It's morning now. Despite still feeling weak from hunger and having a terrible headache from thirst, there is an anger boiling within me. It helped me write all of this down. It's helping me plan my next move.

Whoever reads this – if there are no more words after today, you'll know it's because my attempt to escape has failed. And if it's a villager reading this, you can go to hell. I'll be waiting for you there.

13th DECEMBER

Yesterday morning I heard footsteps, and I considered the possibility that someone was in the house with me.

It's an old house and it creaks a lot, so it could have just been the floorboards shifting. The idea of William getting a round-the-clock guard for me seemed unlikely. This is Morkwood after all, a tiny village obsessed with old laws and fearful of superstitious nonsense. The community wasn't that organised. This wasn't some far-reaching conspiracy backed by money or any substantial power, this was William lording over a group of ignorant countryside folk who didn't know any better.

Plus, I wasn't *that* important.

Yet they had tortured me. And kept me trapped in my own home. And taken Aunt Iris.

Either way, breaking out through the window seemed the only option at this point. I just had to do it quietly, in case there *was* anyone outside my bedroom door.

I first tried prising the wooden planks from the window with my hands, but all that did was imbed splinters into my fingertips. I then tried using the heels of various shoes by wedging them between the glass and the wood to loosen them. It didn't work.

Then an idea hit me. I searched my wardrobe and at the bottom of an old bag I found a purse with loose change in it. I took a coin, placed it into the grooves of one of the screws and tried turning.

It was difficult. The coin kept slipping out, causing my knuckles to scrape against the wood until they bled. But eventually I could feel it begin to loosen.

One by one, each of the screws fell to the floor and the planks came away from the wall, allowing morning sunlight to spill into the room. Its warmth energised me.

There was no time to waste, I had to leave as soon as possible. I decided I would somehow get down using the drainpipe and creep around the outskirts of the village to reach the woods. I would head past the lake to see if Aunt Iris was being kept there. If I couldn't find any evidence of her, I would go to one of the neighbouring villages and ask for help.

I pulled open the window and looked down at my front garden. There were many more wreaths gathered in piles on the lawn, all made of various wild and domesticated animals. Squirrels. Guinea pigs. A few cats. A fox or two.

A larger, more elaborate wreath propped up against the front gate caught my eye. At the top of it was a head, but it wasn't the head of an animal.

It was human.

Aunt Iris.

The eyes were milky white. Mouth slack. Skin grey. Hair saturated with blood and tangled in the sticks and twine of the wreath.

I retched and looked away.

My mind started racing with all the things they could have done to her.

Why? For what?

Did they think they could get away with murdering her, just because she'd said she was shtriga?

And then…a numbness overtook me. It was like a switch had been flicked. Instead of imagining the suffering endured by my last living relative, my last moments with her, and her last moments on this earth, I straightened myself up. I turned away from the window completely. I closed my eyes, and I imagined exactly how I would end William's life.

Although I felt numb, I knew I wouldn't be able to get out of the window and pass Aunt Iris when she looked like…looking the way she did…without making my presence known.

So I left the window open, crawled into the cupboard and waited in the dark.

I waited while the barricade was pulled away from my bedroom door.

I waited while thunderous feet stomped into the room and men argued with one another about who had allowed me to escape.

I waited while they fell over each other retreating down the stairs.

I waited a few more minutes, just to be sure they'd gone. Then I crept out of the cupboard and went downstairs to the kitchen. I forced myself to drink and eat as much as my body could take, even though nausea had replaced my hunger.

I then shut and locked every window. I used my two sofas and the dining table to block the front and back doors. I used the planks of wood from the upstairs window and broke down a few bookshelves to nail wood across all of the downstair windows.

And now? Now I'm going to wait a little longer.

14th DECEMBER

It didn't take long for them to realise what I'd done.

"Margaret! Open up!"

I peeked through the curtain. William was in the front garden with a megaphone. A few men milled around the house carrying an assortment of tools. I could see Arthur and Henry amongst them...even Terry.

I quickly stepped back, not wanting to see Aunt Iris again.

"You need to let us in, Margaret."

I imagined the life leaving William's eyes.

"You can't go anywhere, you do know that, right? I'll give you a few hours to come to your senses, but then we're coming in."

"That's fine with me," I said quietly to myself.

A few hours are all I need.

15th DECEMBER

Yesterday, as William waited for me to welcome him into my house with open arms, I packed a bag with a few clothes and a knife from the kitchen. I listened, ready to move when he moved.

A few hours later, as promised, he ordered some of the villagers to break in. The house was surrounded, but the first and loudest noises came from the back. I grabbed a meat cleaver from the knife block and crouched down close enough to be within swinging distance, but far enough away so that I could jump back to protect myself.

Some sort of loud electric tool was being used to break through the door, so I banked on having the element of surprise. That was my only advantage.

It didn't take long for the flimsy door to break. The sofa blocking it was pushed forward as the door clattered inward onto the tiled floor. The first thing that came into view was a chainsaw, followed by gloved hands and a black puffer jacket.

My only thoughts were of survival.

I lunged forward with the cleaver raised high above my head and hacked down into the side of the intruder's neck. I yanked the cleaver out, ready to use again, but hot blood spurted in all directions, covering the walls, the floor, me. I automatically dropped the cleaver and held my arm in front of my face to protect my eyes.

I heard the chainsaw hit the floor. As I brought my arm back down, it was Dan's startled face I saw.

I ran out the door. I didn't stop to help him. I didn't even see him fall; I just heard a wet smack on the kitchen tiles.

I had to survive.

Every face I saw as I sprinted towards the garden gate was young. Too young. They were all boys from the village – Paul, Jack, Warren – not one of them over the age of sixteen.

They all backed away when they saw me. God knows what I must have looked like. Their shocked eyes followed me as I pulled open the back gate and ran towards the woods, the wreath of Aunt Iris but a blur in the corner of my eye.

I don't know how long I ran for. I couldn't have got very far. All I remember is seeing an unlocked woodshed and, when I turned and saw that no one was behind me, running straight inside. Hiding is my best chance of survival.

I've been telling myself this is survival. I am surviving, I have *survived*. But what am I a survivor of? Dan? He wasn't a killer.

I am.

If I had acted sooner, if I had planned things more carefully, Dan could have left this place and had a better life somewhere else with his family. He was so young. I'm just a crazy, ageing librarian with no family, no friends, no hope. I've never left Morkwood and I'm never going to, no matter how much I kid myself that I will. My roots are too firmly embedded to be able to pull them up now.

Maybe my fate should be placed in the hands of the villagers of Morkwood.

Maybe tomorrow I'll hand myself over to them.

Or maybe I'll keep running.

I don't know. I don't *know*.

I just need to sleep. I'm so tired.

16th DECEMBER

The woodshed was like a cocoon. I felt secure in it, breathing in the earthy smells and blanketed by its surprising warmth. It was as if the stacks of logs were living creatures, all cosily sleeping the winter away with me. It made me feel protected from Morkwood. From William. Maybe even from myself. In this cocoon I could almost forget what I did.

I remained there late into the afternoon, and I could have stayed even longer. But I was lured out by the smell of burning.

I slowly opened the door to thick, black smoke moving across the darkening sky. When I checked my watch, I wasn't surprised to see it was just past four o'clock.

The fire was coming from the Advent House, and I knew exactly what door had been opened.

It was time to give myself over to them. I had thought about it all night, and although leaving Morkwood may have been a possibility once, it isn't something I can do now. I have allowed myself to be swept up in the madness for too long, which means I've helped it to endure. I'd rather face William and make sure the reality of this tradition is seen by as many villagers as possible than slip away in silence.

Thinking back, I had many opportunities to make a stand against the Morkwood way of life. I could have stepped in to help during the numerous times villagers were banished. Mr and Mrs Lawson,

Nicholas, Deidre, Helena, the Frederickson family, and even Sally just a few months ago this summer. All were forced to leave with nothing, their livelihoods taken away, their savings drained, their belongings destroyed.

And then there were the many other traditions I could have refused to participate in. Yes, Christmas was by far the worst, but what about the season changes? The dances? And, my god…the First Blood.

I remember my own First Blood at thirteen, and how humiliating it had been. Yet I hadn't wanted to stop it. I even relished seeing other girls going through it, because that meant my pain hadn't been meaningless.

I don't deserve to be free from something I have helped strengthen.

I'll stop running. I'll allow Morkwood to pass judgement on me in any way they see fit, but I have to try and reason with them first. I want to try and set *them* free.

I followed the smoke to the huge bonfire they'd lit a short distance from the Advent House. I imagined the painting that had instigated it – thick orange and yellow flames that took up most of the canvas, and to the left a man wearing old-fashioned farming clothes holding a piglet by one of its trotters. Lady Greville had even thought to paint blackened, singed hairs on the pig's back where it had been held too close to the blaze.

They were standing around the bonfire when I got there. Every villager over the age of fifteen held a sacrifice, either in their arms or attached to them by rope. There were many farm animals, but for those who didn't own any or couldn't afford to buy them, there were smaller animals – cats, dogs and domesticated rodents. Roderick even held a small fishbowl; his young son, Albert, was crying loudly by his feet.

I thought of the rabbit I had planned to pick up this morning from a pet shop a few miles away. I imagined it sleeping in its hutch, completely unaware that it had narrowly escaped the festivities of Morkwood.

As I watched the villagers stare into the fire, I felt like I was truly seeing Morkwood for the first time. I had always felt like an outsider, but I had never felt so disconnected before. It was almost as though I was looking at my past self.

"What are you all doing?"

The words had fallen from my mouth before I even knew I was speaking.

The only response was blank faces. In the corner of my eye, I saw William nudge a few men and nod in my direction, one of whom was Arthur. I didn't have long.

"What are you all doing?" I asked again. "You're standing in front of a fire like barbarians, and for what? *Why* do we do this, year after year after year?"

I spotted Donald trying to calm his retired sheepdog, who was pulling away from the heat of the fire.

"Are you really going to do this to Samson, Donald? And Roderick, your son is crying, *look* at him. You're about to burn his pet alive. All of you, look at yourselves. It doesn't have to be like this. We can stop all of this."

William took another few steps towards me with four or five men in tow. I began to back away.

"He killed my Aunt Iris, and you all know she wasn't the first. She won't be the last if you don't listen to me and help me stop him. Any of you could be next!"

The men edged closer.

"There are things some of you don't know, too. Ask your husbands what they did on the fifth in the village hall instead of repairing it. Asking your fathers, your sons, they were all…"

With a nod from William, Arthur threw back his arm and punched me hard above my left eye. I didn't feel any pain, but an abrupt dizziness forced me to the ground. Arthur threw himself on top of me to hold me in place.

"You see this?" William yelled, his voice cracking with false emotion. "This is the shtriga who murdered Daniel Hewitt. She's bargaining for her life. Do you deny the murder, shtriga?"

Joan and Harold Hewitt emerged from the crowd. Joan was sobbing. Harold's hands were balled into fists, his face purpling with fury.

"You can see the truth in its eyes." William said. "The evil runs in the family. Remove it from my sight please, Arthur."

Arthur got up, grabbed my foot and pulled me away through the mud. I closed my eyes to the cacophony of screams as, one by one, the animals were tossed into the flames.

17th DECEMBER

I don't know where I am.

I allowed Arthur to pull me across the ground for a short while, just to get me away from the sound of the animals, but when I tried to get up Arthur wasted no time in punching me in the face again. While stunned, he bound my hands and tied a cloth around my face so I couldn't see where we were going.

He didn't bother to untie me when we reached our destination, just pushed me inside a small wooden shed. His knots were loose, and it didn't take long for me to free myself. Not that I can do anything in here – it's dark, and he bolted the door from the outside.

Arthur guarded the door for a few hours, then someone else came to relieve him.

I still have my bag, so I have clothes and a knife, and I have this diary. I found a narrow shaft of light through a crack in the wall, so I can just about see well enough to write.

It smells coppery in here. Like blood.

18th DECEMBER

The door to the shed opened in the early hours of this morning. I was expecting William. I wasn't sure what I was going to say to him – whether to beg, argue, throw logic at him, or just scream – but it wasn't him. It was Gerald, Stuart and Terry. Terry's eyes were bloodshot, and in his trembling hands was a bundle of rope. Gerald held a dining chair that looked as though it had been used as a cat scratching post.

Stuart had a pair of pliers.

I darted towards the door, but there wasn't room to get past all three men. I was shoved and I tripped backwards over my bag. I thrust my hands inside it and grabbed the knife, but Stuart quickly kicked it out of my hand and tucked it into his belt.

Gerald forced me to sit on the chair while Terry tied me to it. His knots were not like Arthur's. As Terry pulled the rope tight it burned and pinched my skin, and I knew there was no way I was getting out of it.

Terry stood back to survey his work and sighed.

"Shut up, Terry," Stuart said, but he didn't sound very convincing. I took the uncertainty in his voice as an opportunity to appeal to his better nature.

"Why are you doing this?" I asked. "Do you not see how insane all of this is? You're holding me hostage in a shed, and what are you going to do now? Torture me?"

Stuart shrugged. "We need information."

I laughed. "What information could I possibly give you? If you need help with a library book, I'm afraid you're going about it the wrong way. Or maybe you think I'm a spy? Perhaps I'm a mole or a secret agent, born here as part of some elaborate, covert mission to share the secrets of Morkwood with the Russians?"

Gerald stepped forward and slapped me across the face. It felt like a tendon in my neck ripped with the force of it.

Stuart rubbed his eyes with the heels of his hands. "I apologise on Gerald's behalf for that, but we do need information. We don't want to be here. We've got a lot to do on the farm before the snow settles, so as you can imagine we're not in the best of moods. It would serve you well to tell us everything you know as quickly as you can."

I sat still for a moment, my face still stinging from the slap. "I honestly don't know what you want from me. Just let me go and I'll leave the village, I won't tell anyone what has gone on here. I'll just go."

Stuart held the pliers near my face so I could see them up close. They smelled of oil and rust.

"Just tell us what you know."

"About what?"

"About the shtriga."

A buried memory resurfaced of a rough pencil drawing on the back of a notebook. As children, we used to sketch the pointed face, hideous, soulless eyes and coarse, long hair of the shtriga onto each other's schoolwork. She always had sharp teeth and branch-like fingers.

The shtriga is featured in many of the stories told in Morkwood. Some of the smaller details about her vary, depending on the storyteller, but there's one thing that always remains the same; the shtriga hunts for children in the dead of night to drain them of their blood. It's the only way she can fuel her witchcraft.

If any child under the age of five dies in Morkwood, the shtriga is immediately blamed – partly to hold something accountable for such a senseless tragedy, but also because the villagers genuinely believe in her. No one talks about her seriously beyond the age of twelve, but no one dismisses her either. To do so would be bad luck. It would be like daring the shtriga to visit you.

I started to tell the three men what I knew. What legends I had heard, what the shtriga looked like... but Stuart cut me off.

"I don't want stories," he said, "I want information."

"I'm telling you everything I know."

"No, I don't want to hear about the *idea* of shtriga. I want to hear about *the* shtriga. Your aunt."

I looked at each of them, searching for a clue as to what this was really about. But they seemed serious.

"William and Arthur murdered my aunt," I said.

"You can't murder the shtriga," Stuart said.

I thought of my aunt's decapitated head. Milky white eyes. Slack mouth. Grey, blood-drained flesh. Her frozen expression of pain and anguish.

I felt desperately tired. More tired than I felt miserable, or hopeless, or angry. The exhaustion was settling in my bones, making me feel heavy and slow.

"Just do it, then," I said. "Whatever it is you're going to do, just do it."

Terry stepped forward, crouched down to my level and put my hands on my knees. His brow was furrowed.

"Please, Margaret, tell us where she is so we can catch her. There are children to think about. *Please*."

They're insane. They're all completely insane.

"She's *dead*!" I shouted. "William murdered her. She was just a woman, a normal decent human being, and he drowned her and cut off her head because she said she was shtriga. I don't know why she did that, I don't know why he killed her, and I don't know why we have to try and find a witch every Christmas, but that's it. That's all there is to this. What else am I supposed to know?"

"Where is she, Margaret?" Stuart asked.

"You know where she is. She was cut up and dumped on my front lawn."

I began to cry then. It was almost joyful, the release it gave me. I let myself sob from the depths of my stomach, my entire body shuddering with the sheer force of it.

"I don't think she knows," Terry said, turning to Stuart.

"She's pretending," Stuart said. "This is all a trick."

Terry shook his head and turned back to me. "Margaret, she's gone," he said.

"I know she's dead."

"Not dead. *Gone.* Her body is gone. And they found Carla Harris' baby in her place at your house. The shtriga drained him of all blood. She reformed."

I slumped in the chair, shaking my head at the bizarre lies spewing from their mouths.

Stuart pulled Terry onto his feet and pushed him aside.

"You know what that means, don't you, Margaret?" Stuart leaned in close. "It means someone took Carla's baby and offered him to the shtriga so she could rise up from the dead."

"And you think I did it," I said, laughing a little in disbelief.

19th DECEMBER

I can barely write. I'm shaking too much.

Yesterday, after questioning me for hours and ignoring all of my answers, Terry, Stuart and Gerald finally released me from the chair. Someone else brought food and water, but I couldn't see their face in the dark. I was forced to toilet in the corner of the shed.

They left me all night. I somehow managed to sleep, using my bag as a pillow.

When the three of them returned this morning, no words were spoken. They simply forced me onto the chair again, bound my legs together and tied my right arm behind my back.

When Gerald pulled the pliers out of his pocket, I didn't say anything. I thought it was another empty threat.

But then he pinched the base of my left thumb. He held the end of the nail with the pliers. And before I had the chance to struggle, he yanked the pliers upwards, tearing the nail off.

The burning, throbbing pain is unlike anything I've felt before.

They untied me in silence and left.

They deserve to have their babies taken from them. I want them all to suffer for what they've done.

20th DECEMBER

I keep hearing the noise of my nail tearing from my thumb, over and over in my head.

I wrapped the thumb in a handkerchief I found in my bag. It stopped bleeding, but I don't want to look at it. I know it's bad. It feels bad. It hasn't stop throbbing since it happened, not for a single moment.

It's going to get infected. I'm going to die because of these moronic villagers.

I should have left when I had the chance. I was fifteen when my father died. My mother suggested we leave to start a new life somewhere. She said we could move to a town or even a city, I could get a better education and she could get a better job.

But I didn't want to lose my friends. My familiarity. My routine. I cut the outside world off because I was scared of the unknown.

And now I'm scared of everything I know.

I found my thumbnail while scrabbling around on the floor this morning, delirious and tired from the pain. I started to play with it by bending it in half, scraping the stringy, bloody skin from underneath it.

Then I put it in my pocket. It feels important to keep it. A keepsake.

The door opened while I was dozing. Someone placed cold, stewed vegetables and a glass of milk on the floor for me. I gagged it all down and fell asleep again.

As the day came and went and the light outside began to fade, I realised they wouldn't come back for me today.

Through a small gap in the door, I could see a man guarding the shed. His back was to me. I tried speaking to him. He didn't even flinch.

Then I heard a rustling.

I turned to see a shockingly white square in the middle of the dark, damp floor.

A piece of paper.

I picked it up and turned it over.

I'll come for you soon.

I tucked the sheet of paper in between some clothes in my bag. I need to read it again tomorrow, just to know I haven't made it up. Just so I know I'm not still asleep.

21st DECEMBER

It's an odd feeling, to suspect your own relative of being shtriga.

I thought about it all night. As a product of Morkwood's superstitions, part of me can't help but think Aunt Iris rose from the dead and left me that note. I grew up on stories of mothers finding nothing but droplets of blood in their baby's cribs, and of villagers making pacts with the devil by offering their firstborn to the shtriga. It's hard to separate myself from all that.

As a teenager, I provoked and tested the fears I had been brought up with by going into the woods late at night with friends, carving symbols into trees and calling upon the evil spirits to show themselves. Nothing happened, so I came to the conclusion that it was all nonsense. And I had continued believing that into adulthood.

For the most part...but there was always doubt.

The piece of paper is still in my bag. It is *real*. But how did it get in here, if not by forces unknown?

I'm only given one meal a day in here. Milk and cold vegetable stew. It makes me nauseous – I can feel the foamy, tangy drink and thick, brown mush curdling inside of me. I feel weak and my mind drifts from one thing to the next, never quite able to grab hold of any thought long enough to properly contemplate what's going on, or what to do.

It's also getting increasingly difficult to separate my dreams from my imagination. Or what has happened from what I want to happen. Or where I want to be, from where I actually am.

I peeled the handkerchief from my thumb. It's red and swollen and sore, but it doesn't hurt as much as it did yesterday. I ripped one of the sleeves off a clean t-shirt from my bag and rewrapped the wound. I have to keep it clean. God knows what's in this shed. I wish they'd give me water so I could wash it.

I want to sleep all the time. But I can't sleep.

I'm going to die in here.

—

I must have dozed again. A few minutes? A few hours? I don't know, but it was a knock on the door that woke me.

I thought maybe I imagined it but no, it continued. Slow and deliberate.

I crawled over to the door with one hand, my sore thumb held close to my chest. My mind was too foggy to work out how to stand, and I didn't trust my legs to support me.

I peered through the crack in the wood. I could see the guard, and he was facing the opposite direction, but his hand was behind his back, knocking on the door.

"Hello?" I whispered, my voice cracking.

He stopped knocking.

After a short pause, he spoke very, very quietly. "Tomorrow."

"What's tomorrow?"

"Be ready."

"Ready for what? What do I need to do?"

But he didn't respond, and his hand slowly returned to his side.

I've had my doubts, but now I'm certain. My aunt must have possessed the guard. She spoke to me through him.

She's coming for me tomorrow. She's coming to save me.

22nd DECEMBER

I'm sitting in an armchair by a warm fire, drinking hot chocolate with a dash of whisky, eating mince pies. To stop myself from weeping with joy, I've started to write.

Last night, in a state of delirium, I kept myself awake for fear of missing my aunt. I didn't know which form she would take when she came to rescue me, whether it would be through a guard or an animal. I've heard shtriga commonly appear as crows, so I tried to listen out for a caw or a pecking at the door.

But I couldn't keep my eyes open. I fell into a deep, heavy sleep, and only woke when I felt my arm being lifted upwards.

I smiled, thinking my sleeve was being tugged by a narrow black beak, but when I opened my eyes I saw that it was actually a hand. A man's hand.

My bleary vision cleared. Terry was leaning over me, trying to get me to stand.

"Come on," he said, "we need to go. *Now.*"

I clambered to my feet.

"Aunt Iris?"

He stopped pulling at me for a moment. "What? No, Margaret, it's Terry. Can you see me? Are you alright?"

I rubbed my eyes and tried to gather my bearings.

"You're not Aunt Iris?"

"Can you see?"

"Yes, yes, I just thought…"

"Did you get my note? I stuck it to your back as we left so Stuart and Gerald wouldn't see it."

I felt both relieved and ridiculous all at once, but then… uncertainty took hold. I'm not sure if it was the hunger, the exhaustion or everything I've been through over the past few weeks, but I couldn't quite get my head around the idea that it was Terry rescuing me, not my Aunt Iris.

Perhaps it *was* her, and she didn't think I could handle the idea of my own aunt being shtriga. Perhaps I was still asleep.

"We need to *go*," Terry insisted.

I pushed aside my questions and grabbed my bag.

Terry opened the door and stepped over the body of a man. My faceless guard. As I neared him, I saw that it was Marcus. I didn't know him very well, but I know he was a friend of Arthur's. There was a deep cut across his throat and his eyes were open and flat. His blood had soaked into the earth around his head.

Terry saw me hesitate.

"I had no choice," he said.

"Why are you helping me?"

"Because it's the right thing to do."

If this was a fairy tale, my aunt would have chosen that moment to take off the mask she had cast onto herself, but of course that didn't happen. I had to stop believing in their stories. The Morkwood lies. She was dead.

I lumbered behind Terry as he ran to his truck, which was parked on a lane a few metres from the shed. As my eyes adjusted to the dark, I realised where we were. Arthur's back garden. He was probably still in his house somewhere.

The thought of waking him terrified me.

Aside from the sound of our feet squelching in the mud, we managed to get into the truck and close the doors without making much noise. When Terry started the engine, my teeth sank into my tongue and I gripped tightly onto the seats.

But no lights came on in the house. There was no shouting, no shotguns firing in the dark. We were leaving. We were getting away.

Terry drove slowly up the lane and onto the main road. I wanted to tell him to go faster, but I knew it would wake the village up if he did. Instead, I sank down as far as I could and closed my eyes. My fate was in his hands.

After ten minutes or so, Terry parked the truck. I opened my eyes.

"We're at your house," I said.

"Yes."

"Are you insane? We need to get out of Morkwood."

"Not yet. William has people on the road leading out of the village."

"So what exactly is your plan?"

"I'm going to hide you in my attic."

"You *are* insane."

Terry shifted in his seat and rested his hands on my knees, as he had done in the shed a couple of days ago. He was uncomfortably close to me. If he hadn't had an expression of pure fear on his face, I would have squirmed away from him.

"You have to trust me," he said, tears welling in his eyes. "I know what will happen if we try to leave. We won't stand a chance. We need to make William think he's won. If you lie low for a couple of days, he'll send people out to look for you. By Christmas Eve, when he can't find you and the police don't come, he'll think you're well clear of Morkwood. And then…"

He let go of me and leant back, wiping his eyes with the back of his hand.

"And then what?" I asked.

He took a deep breath. "And then we show Morkwood the truth. We have to at least try. If we don't, they'll just help him cover the whole thing up."

"But what is the truth? Why is William doing all of this?"

"I asked Father Hundyke that very question a week ago. He said, 'If you suffer for doing good and you endure it, this is commendable before God.' Perhaps William thinks the more we suffer, the more protected we'll be from the shtriga."

I said nothing. The idea that William is doing this to protect the souls of the villagers from the devil is a crazier notion than me thinking my dead aunt had possessed Terry's body.

In the house, I poured myself glass after glass of fresh, cold, clean water from the tap, while Terry cooked me a meal of eggs,

85

toast and sausages. He then ran a bath so hot I could barely stand it, but I sat in the water and scrubbed at my body until my skin was raw. I then bandaged my thumb and put on new clothes. I felt almost human again.

I spent the rest of the day in Terry's attic. I slept mostly, waking once around midday to find more water and food had been left for me. It was a slight upgrade from being locked in the shed.

At five o'clock, Terry came up to announce that dinner was ready. We sat in his dining room and ate boiled potatoes and trout in complete silence. Terry didn't look like he wanted to talk, but once we were finished I couldn't help myself.

"Do they know I've escaped?"

He nodded. "They're searching for you. I spent two hours in the woods this afternoon helping them look."

He got up from the table and opened a cabinet. Inside were bottles of whisky and homebrewed, unlabelled beer. He poured a couple of fingers of whisky into two glasses and handed me one.

"I still don't know why you helped me," I said. I gulped down half of my drink, enjoying the warmth in my chest and on my cheeks.

Terry sighed. "I've felt – *uncomfortable* – about living here for some time. When they did what they did to Iris, I tried to think of a way out, but it's difficult. They know too much."

"What do you mean? What do they know?"

Terry ignored my questions. "And things got worse when you stopped going to the Advent House. William has been hard on people, and there have been consequences for anyone who refuses him."

"Consequences?"

"That's what he's calling it. I don't know everything that's been happening, but what I do know is awful. Really awful." He took a deep breath. "I think he took that baby and made it look like your aunt was shtriga. He knew the village were on the edge of rebelling against him, but they're now terrified of the shtriga coming for their children. They think you're shtriga and that you killed Marcus. They're scared of you too."

I felt sick. "You're risking too much keeping me here. They'll think I bewitched you and I'm using your body like a puppet for my own bidding."

He shrugged. "I have nothing to lose."

Terry's wife died of cancer six months ago, and all three of his children left Morkwood as soon as they were able to. I don't think he has much contact with them.

"Right," I said, getting up and grabbing the whisky from the cabinet. "Tonight we're going to drink the rest of this. And tomorrow we work out what the hell we're going to do."

23rd DECEMBER

With food and rest, my thinking has become clearer. My anger is returning.

Memories are returning to me as well. Memories of William banning Jacob from purchasing alcohol for life after witnessing him vomit on his eighteenth birthday. Memories of William marching Annie off somewhere in the middle of Easter Sunday lunch and returning without her, all because she dropped a cake. Memories of Roberta falling down a flight of stairs minutes after William had said her shoes made her look like a whore.

And then there was Frederick Hughes.

I had heard the post office 'let go' of Frederick because there wasn't enough work for him to do, but no one knows the full story. Some say he was asked to leave for taking too many sick days. Others insist he was a pervert and was fired after a complaint from a customer.

Either way, when he left the post office he was in his late sixties and couldn't find another job. After eight months his savings completely dried up, and he began to ask locals for small loans.

It soon became clear he wasn't able to pay anyone back, so they stopped lending him money. Frederick begged for food instead. When William found out about it, he told Frederick he was an embarrassment to Morkwood and needed to stop. He couldn't, and didn't.

One afternoon I was walking home from work when I saw Frederick loitering outside of the greengrocers near closing time, waiting to take something unsellable off of Wallace's hands. Then William approached him.

"I'll buy you a full week's worth of groceries," William had said, "but you have to do something for me first."

Frederick's face lit up. "Of course, anything, just let me know what you need."

I remember William's expression vividly. He lowered his gaze, and his lips pulled back into an animalistic snarl. I half expected him to leap forward and bite into Frederick's neck.

William took a deep breath, as if the next thing he was going to say would pain him terribly. "I'll trade you a week's worth of food for your clothes."

"What clothes?" Frederick asked.

"The ones you're wearing."

Frederick laughed nervously and turned to onlookers for reassurance. Everyone who was there, myself included, said nothing. Yet no one left. We all just kept watching.

"If you don't strip in the next minute, the deal is over." William looked down at his watch. "Fifty-five seconds... Fifty... Forty-five..."

Frederick pulled his shirt off and began unbuttoning his trousers. At that point I looked away and went home.

Two days later, Frederick Hughes was found hanging in his bathroom.

No one questioned it. No one blamed William. It was just something that happened, and it was never spoken of again.

It's strange. I was once able to accept so much, to look away from so much, until suddenly I couldn't anymore. There was a time when I would have done anything for normalcy and anonymity, but then one day it all appeared both absurd and impossible, and I realised I was drenched in guilt.

I've come to realise that most people believe they're independent thinkers who are vehemently true to themselves. In reality, we're all susceptible to the voice of authority and the appearance of confidence. We're all sheep. Cowards. We're not the star of the show, we're the background characters that keep the world chugging forward.

Because William owns the biggest property and most of the land in the village, has a renowned lineage and chairs numerous local councils and committees, he is seen. He is believed. We give him power, and we allow him to take more of it.

I remember William's father, Victor. He was similar to his son insofar as he relished cruelty, but he had a very different approach to it. William likes one-on-one interactions and honing in on the vulnerable. Victor got other people to do his dirty work for him. He always took a step back from the villagers, but he always enjoyed watching the results of his commands.

Victor didn't allow women to attend church alone. Victor kicked anyone out of the village who had a child out of wedlock. Victor banned books that didn't ascribe to Morkwood values.

Victor also bashed his wife's skull in with an ornamental musket – although no one would dare to say that too loudly in Morkwood. The official report stated she died of a brain aneurism and had fallen down the stairs, but Mrs Lassiter used to clean for the Grevilles and had been the one who found her. She told everyone she had found Lady Eunice Greville in the living room.

Victor dismissed it and said Mrs Lassiter was clearly upset and confused, and that was that. Another death that Morkwood collectively hid from outsiders.

But the Harris' baby will be the final secret of the Grevilles' one-hundred-and-fifty-year curse.

Thirty minutes ago, Terry and I discussed our plans. We agreed that talking is not going to release the villagers of Morkwood from over a century of suspicion, lies and autocracy.

The only thing they'll listen to, and the only thing they've ever listened to, is fear.

24th DECEMBER

The twenty-fourth door of the Advent House is always the same. The big feast.

The ceremony starts at midday, with twenty-four live turkeys being placed into each of the doors of the Advent House. They remain in there while the village sings, eats, drinks and exchanges gifts.

At around four o'clock, the villagers stand twenty-four paces from the Advent House, facing the opposite direction. One by one, William releases the turkeys. When he rings the bell, the villagers can turn around to try and grab a turkey. Whoever manages to catch and kill one can keep it for their Christmas Day dinner.

Terry and I are going to arrive before the killing of the turkeys. By then the villagers will be merry and relaxed. William won't expect it. It's the perfect time to strike.

Our plan is simple. We approach from the woods to where William is sitting – at the left-hand side of the Advent House, facing the villagers, as he always does – and we'll hold him at gunpoint. We'll make sure no one is close by, then Terry will shoot him in the face.

We considered forcing William to tell the villagers the truth, that the shtriga isn't real, that he killed Carla's baby, but Terry and I agreed it would be easier to kill him. We'll most likely get killed ourselves, and at the very least arrested, but if we don't do this the festivities of Morkwood will continue.

No more William Greville.

No more Advent House.

No more Christmas.

–

I can hear sirens in the distance. I can also hear the frantic shouts of the villagers, pleading for help to no one in particular, lost in blind panic. I'm going to have to block it all out so I can write, but once I've finished, I'll hand myself over to them. I just need to get this out of my head.

At about one o'clock, Terry and I approached the Advent House from the woods as planned, but as we got closer we couldn't hear any of the usual chatter we would expect from the big feast. No glasses clinked together. Music played, but underneath was a cold, heavy silence.

Terry and I exchanged worried looks. Something was definitely wrong, but there was no turning back now.

When we got to the clearing it certainly looked like a typical Christmas Eve. William sat in his fold-out chair to the side of the Advent House, eating a sandwich from a lunchbox. The tables and chairs used for outdoor events had been set out across the grass, and the villagers had food and drink in front of them, yet not a single plate had been touched.

There was no time to revise our plan. Terry took a deep breath and marched straight up to William, aiming his gun at the side of his head. I followed a few paces behind.

"Stand up, William," Terry demanded. It was a tone I hadn't heard in his voice before.

William stood slowly, raising his hands above his head. When he turned around, he looked over Terry's shoulder and smiled at me.

"We've been waiting for you, Margaret," he said. "We saved a seat for you."

Terry prodded William's forehead with the gun. "Shut up."

As I opened my mouth to speak, there was a loud crack. It felt close, as if a firework had been let off at my feet.

I jumped back, clutching my ringing ears. I assumed Terry had shot William, but William was still standing with his hands above his head, smiling at me. Only now there was blood splattered across the side of his face.

Terry slumped to his knees, one hand instinctively holding his neck to stem the bleeding. He fell face-first into the ground.

Over my shoulder, I saw Arthur inching slowly towards Terry, his handgun still pointed at him. After booting him in the side, Arthur picked up Terry's gun and tossed it aside.

Then he turned his gun on me.

"Should I let them out now?" Arthur asked William, although his eyes remained fixed on me.

William checked his watch. "No, it's still far too early, and no one has finished their lunch yet. Just put her in the last door and we'll let them all out in a couple of hours."

He seemed strangely focused for a man who'd just had a gun pointed at his head. I looked back at the Advent House – all of the doors were closed except for the twenty-fourth, three rows from the bottom.

"What's going on?" I asked.

"When there is shtriga in Morkwood, the birds are not enough," William said matter-of-factly.

"What? What does that mean? What have you done, William?"

He sighed, as if he couldn't be bothered to explain such a simple concept to me. "I do so much to keep them away. I work so hard, just as my ancestors did, to keep them satisfied, to keep all of you safe, but the shtriga are like a stain. There are still some remnants of your aunt here, even though I did everything right. Surely you can feel her still? Taste her in the air? It hasn't helped that you and Terry, God rest his soul, have worked so hard to carry out her bidding.

"So to be truly clean, to be properly rid of the shtriga at the most dangerous time of the year, Morkwood needs to give her a gift that will satisfy her in the Otherworld. She needs the souls of men."

The villagers were expressionless, their eyes trained on their uneaten food. I wanted them to look up at me, to help me understand what was really going on.

That's when I noticed the empty chairs.

The kitchen knives, screwdrivers, axes and hammers laid at their feet under the tables.

The twenty-three closed doors.

And I knew what they were prepared to do for Morkwood. For tradition. For superstition. For William.

But the Advent House, why was it so silent? When it's filled with turkeys the noise is deafening. The birds can sense what's about to happen to them and they panic, throwing themselves against the walls of their prison until they half-kill themselves. Why were the people inside not screaming for help? Had they offered their lives *willingly*?

Maybe there was no helping Morkwood.

But there was no helping me either.

Arthur pistol-whipped me across the temple and I collapsed to my hands and knees, seeing an amalgamation of swirls of darkness and sparkles of light. I was vaguely aware of being dragged onto the cherrypicker and pushed inside an advent door, but my brain couldn't connect with my body.

With the door closed I was in true, impenetrable darkness. Inside the Advent House it smelled like sawdust, and something acidic. I lay in the foetal position facing the inside of the door, waiting for the pain in my head to subside and my thoughts to come together. I needed another plan.

Maybe William had lied. Maybe there was no one in the house but me.

I knocked on the wood beneath me.

"Is anyone there?" I whispered.

Silence.

But then…a whimper. It was very quiet, and could have easily been made by an animal.

"Is someone there?"

I heard the whimper again, but muffled. As if someone had clamped their hand over their mouth.

"You don't need to die. Do you hear me? We can get out of here, just knock to let me know you can hear me. We can do this together."

The whimpering stopped.

I kicked the door a few times, but it wouldn't budge. I tried slapping the floor to get someone's attention, and I rapped on the walls and ceiling with my knuckles. No one responded. There were twenty-three other people in that house, all obediently waiting for death.

There was something about their compliance that fuelled my anger. With a yell I slammed my heel towards the back of the house…and my foot tore through the painted canvas. Daylight illuminated my boxy prison.

I rolled slowly over. Through the ripped painting of a turkey, I could see there was about a metre of space between the back of the Advent House and the side of William's manor house. The light was coming from above. Below there was nothing but mud.

I turned over onto my stomach and slowly pushed both of my feet through the canvas. I then shuffled backwards, allowing the weight of my legs to pull the rest of me out. My stomach lurched as I began to fall – I had underestimated just how far the drop was – and as I landed my ankle twisted awkwardly beneath me.

I sunk my teeth into my lower lip to stifle the scream.

Then I listened.

No shouts. No commotion. All I could hear was the Christmas music.

I stood up and put a little weight on my ankle. The pain made my eyes water, but I could just about hobble on it. Using the walls either side of me for support, I began to limp along the gap between the Advent House and the manor house.

I expected the wood that bridged between the two structures at the end to be solid, but it was so old and thin it cracked from a couple of whacks with my elbow. I pulled it apart with my fingers, bending back the shards of wood until they snapped and created a hole large enough to fit through.

I staggered out and immediately tripped over Terry's gun. It felt like fate. I held it up with trembling hands.

I limped around the side of the Advent House to where William was, still sitting in his chair, with Terry lying face down not far from him. I pushed the gun to the back of William's head.

Seeing his entire body jolt in surprise was the single most joyful thing I have ever witnessed.

"Don't turn around," I said.

"Margaret?"

"Don't you dare turn around. I want them all to see you."

"Margaret, you…"

I pulled the trigger. His whole body spasmed as the hot contents of his skull sprayed into the air.

I looked up to see Arthur running towards me, tugging his handgun free from his belt.

I didn't move, except to loosen my grip on the gun so it would slip from my fingers. I think I would have let him kill me. I might have even wanted him to kill me. But before he was able to get close, the villagers intervened.

Benjamin Wethers rugby tackled him to the ground, while Tracy Pryer kicked his gun out of reach. She held her booted foot in the space above his head, her face contorted in a mixture of determination and pure hate. I turned away.

And collided with someone standing directly behind me.

Terry.

His neck was open, congealed blood covering his face and clothes. His skin greyish white. He was dead, but his eyes weren't. They were bright, alive, *shining* even.

He leaned in close. His breath smelled stale.

"I'm not leaving without my gift."

His voice sounded like Aunt Iris.

Shtriga.

His words were like a switch. I felt something in the air, like a tingling on my skin, and then the Advent House was engulfed in flames. The sheer force of the heat pushed me sideways.

"Merry Christmas, Margaret."

The life left Terry's eyes, and he was face-down on the ground once more.

There was no helping the people inside. The fire was too fierce, too fast. Most of them didn't even get the chance to scream.

I know what everyone will think. They'll think it was me who started the fire. I don't know if they saw Terry, but would it matter if they did? He's dead now. As are William and Arthur. They've all paid for their sins, but the villagers need someone to blame for the fire.

I ran as fast as I was able to. I went straight to Terry's attic, the only place I could think to go. I'm writing my last moments down to complete this diary in the hope that Morkwood will believe me. They'll kill me before I'll be able to explain myself to them, but I want them to find out the truth.

The sirens are getting louder, and I can hear their cries. They're looking for me.

To all my friends and neighbours, I'm sorry. I'm sorry it had to end like this, but at least now we know for sure.

Keep your children close this Christmas.

Because the shtriga is real.

Come on, haste, let us open,
The Advent House doors await.
Wake up the children, wrap up warm,
Quick, best not be late.

For if we delay, no matter why,
The woods will know it first.
The trees will find and claim us,
And our Yule-tide will be curs'd.

And if we refuse the games and folly,
Thoust surely misunderstood.
There is fear in the night for those who scorn
The festivities of Morkwood.

IF YOU ENJOYED THE FESTIVITIES OF MORKWOOD...

E.J. BABB'S DEBUT NOVEL, **THESE UNNATURAL MEN**, IS AVAILABLE ON AMAZON AND KOBO.

This gripping dystopian debut by E.J. Babb is a haunting glimpse into a very possible, very divisive future. With an unflinching exploration into life and living, this is a must for readers of Orwell's *1984*, Huxley's *Brave New World* and Alderman's *the Power*.

The public call her a cold-blooded murderer. An executioner. A killer for hire.

Nieve Hindeman is a euthanasist.

She is one of hundreds of professionals relieving patients of their pain every day. To her, euthanasia is simply a medical solution to a medical problem.

But when Nieve starts to treat a voluntary patient - a man who is physically healthy but choosing to die - she starts to question the work she does. How can she prove that someone's desire to die is genuine? Can a patient ever be psychologically terminally ill? And is a life ever *not* worth saving?

REVIEWS FOR THESE UNNATURAL MEN

"HARD TO PUT DOWN ONCE YOU GET STARTED."

"I COMPLETELY BINGED THIS BOOK IN TWO DAYS."

"CAREFULLY HANDLED AND ADEPTLY CRAFTED."

In 2012, E.J. Babb sought a platform to discuss dystopian fiction – a rather bleak yet hopeful genre – and thus, Dystopic was born.

Dystopic is predominantly dedicated to reviews and discussions on dystopian literature and film, but also includes sci-fi, horror, speculative fiction, dark comedy and non-fiction.

For more information, visit:

www.dystopic.co.uk